STEPHEN BIESTY'S
INCREDIBLE
CROSS-SECTIONS

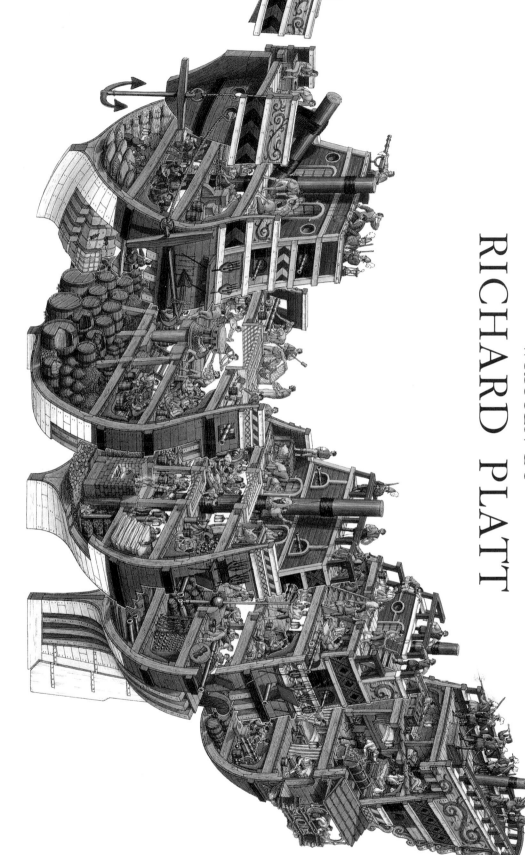

ILLUSTRATED BY
STEPHEN BIESTY

WRITTEN BY
RICHARD PLATT

ALFRED A. KNOPF · NEW YORK

Contents

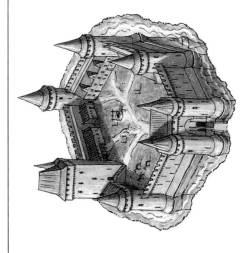
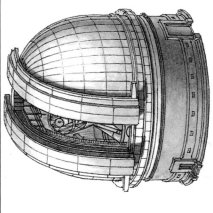

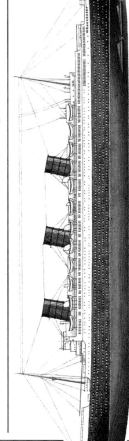

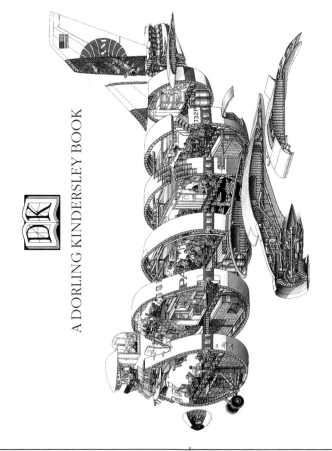

A DORLING KINDERSLEY BOOK

Project Editor John C. Miles
Art Editor Richard Czapnik
Production Marguerite Fenn
Managing Editor Ann Kramer
Art Director Roger Priddy

This is a Borzoi Book published by Alfred A. Knopf, Inc

First American edition, 1992

Copyright © 1992 Dorling Kindersley Limited, London.
All rights reserved under International and Pan-American
Copyright Convention. Published in the United States by
Alfred A. Knopf, Inc., New York. Distributed by Random House,
Inc., New York. Published in Great Britain by
Dorling Kindersley Limited, London.

Manufactured in Italy 0 9 8 7 6 5

Library of Congress Cataloging in Publication Data
Biesty, Stephen.
Stephen Biesty's Incredible Cross-sections
written by Richard Platt;
illustrated by Stephen Biesty.
p. cm
Includes index.
Summary: Cross-sectional illustrations present an inside view of
such structures as a medieval castle, factory, and subway station.
1. Biesty, Stephen.—Themes, motives—Juvenile literature.
2. Interior architecture.—Juvenile literature.
[1.Interior architecture. 2. Architecture.] I. Title.
NC975.5.B5A4 1992
741.642'092—dc20 91-27439
ISBN 0-679-81411-6

Reproduced by Dot Gradations, Essex
Printed and bound in Italy by A. Mondadori Editore, Verona

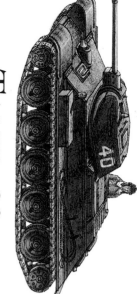
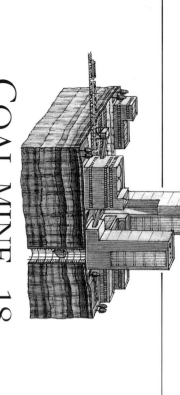
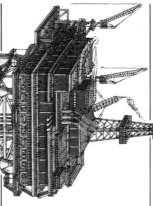
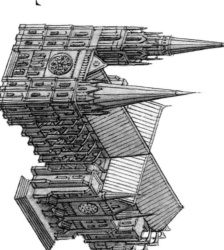

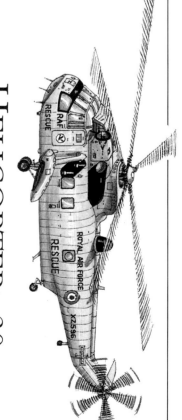

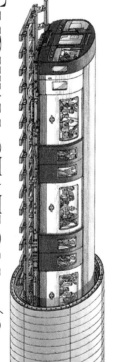
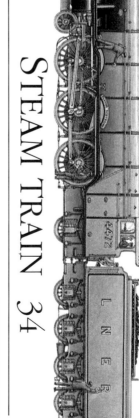
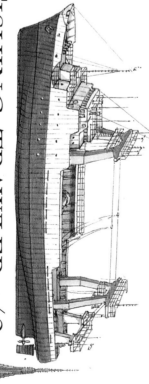

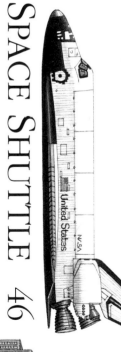

CASTLE

Hundreds of years ago, life in Europe was dangerous and wars were common. So powerful people built castles — strong homes where they could take shelter from their enemies, or launch attacks against them. Usually a nobleman, or lord, owned the castle. The king gave the lord land in return for soldiers to help fight wars. Tenants farmed the lord's land. In return for their labor, they earned enough to live on and were protected in wartime by the lord and his soldiers. Society inside the castle walls mirrored the world outside. The lord and his officials managed the castle and the lands around it. Below the officials in rank were priests, important servants, and soldiers. At the bottom of castle society were the most humble workers, such as laborers and the cesspool cleaner shown below.

Many 14th-century castles had thick outer walls, which enclosed a central open area.

Deadly fire
Narrow slits in the castle walls allowed archers to fire freely, while protecting them from incoming arrows. From the overhang at the top of the walls, defenders could drop stones on attackers' heads to stop them from climbing the walls.

Gatehouse
The only way into the castle was through the gatehouse. This was the weakest point in the castle wall. Defenders on the top of the wall fired arrows at attackers who got too close, or threw boiling water down on them. The defenders could also lower a huge gate, called a portcullis, which trapped their attackers.

Getting inside
Capturing a castle was difficult. Attackers had to try to tunnel under the walls, trick the people inside, or lay siege and starve them out to gain access. Castles were an effective defense until about 350 years ago, when gunpowder came into wide use and attacking armies could easily blow holes in the strongest castle wall.

A moat point
Another defense was a water-filled trench called a moat, which surrounded the castle. The moat was a difficult hurdle for attackers, and also stopped them from digging a tunnel under the walls. The road to the gatehouse crossed the moat by means of a hinged drawbridge, which could be raised.

Doing time
Prisoners were locked up in an underground cell, called a dungeon. Oubliettes, or secret dungeons, got their name from the French word *oublier*, meaning "to forget." Oubliettes were reserved for the most hated prisoners. Their captors locked them up — and forgot about them!

CASTLE PERSONALITIES

Cesspool cleaner   *Priest*   *Noble family*   *Jester*   *Knight*

Commander's quarters

Tiled roof

Food store

On guard
The guards were stationed in this room when on duty. They ate their meals here and warmed themselves near a basket of hot charcoal called a brazier.

Castle guards

Portcullis

Drawbridge

4

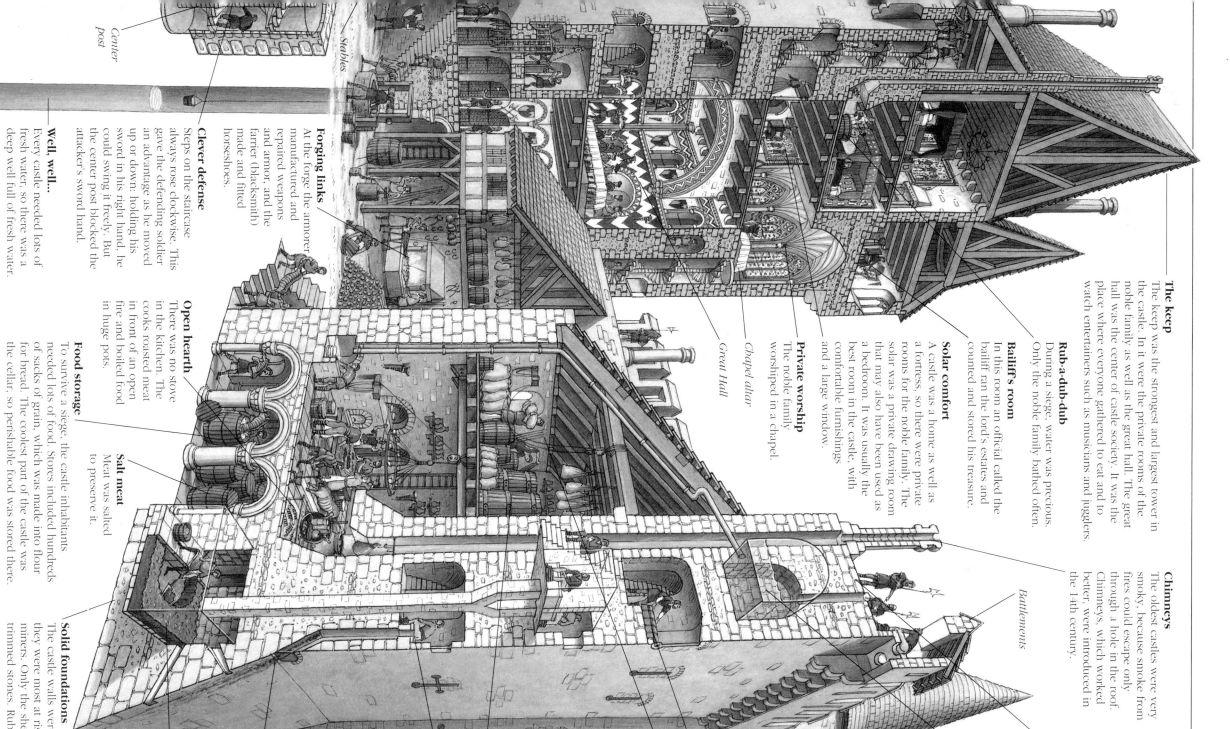

The keep
The keep was the strongest and largest tower in the castle. In it were the private rooms of the noble family as well as the great hall. The great hall was the center of castle society. It was the place where everyone gathered to eat and to watch entertainers such as musicians and jugglers.

Rub-a-dub-dub
During a siege, water was precious. Only the noble family bathed often.

Bailiff's room
In this room an official called the bailiff ran the lord's estates and counted and stored his treasure.

Solar comfort
A castle was a home as well as a fortress, so there were private rooms for the noble family. The solar was a private drawing room that may also have been used as a bedroom. It was usually the best room in the castle, with comfortable furnishings and a large window.

Private worship
The noble family worshiped in a chapel.

Chapel altar

Great Hall

Chimneys
The oldest castles were very smoky, because smoke from fires could escape only through a hole in the roof. Chimneys, which worked better, were introduced in the 14th century.

A walk on the wall
Along the top of the castle wall was a path called a wall walk. It enabled defending soldiers to move quickly around the castle to the point of attack. Stone pillars, or battlements, protected soldiers on the wall walk from enemy arrows.

Cistern
Rainwater from the roofs drained into huge stone tanks called cisterns. Lead pipes took the water to the kitchen.

Wooden shutter
Window glass was not widely used until the 15th century; until then castles were very cold.

Deadly tubes
Soldiers used cannons (heavy guns) from the mid-14th century on. The first cannons were just tubes of metal fixed to stout wooden frames.

Battlements

Cheers!
The beer in a 14th-century castle was very strong — even the "small beer" that children drank was more alcoholic than beer is today. It was brewed often, because 14th-century beer did not keep very well.

Fermenting beer

Solid foundations
The castle walls were thickest at the bottom, where they were most at risk from tunneling by enemy miners. Only the shell of the castle wall was made from trimmed stones. Rubble filled the core of the castle wall.

Splash!
The toilets in castles were very primitive. They were called garderobes. Usually there was just a hole that led to the outside wall. Sewage from some of the garderobes went straight into the moat.

This job's the pits...
Other garderobes in castles emptied into pits called cesspools. Cleaning them out was a very smelly job!

Exit from garderobe

Salt meat
Meat was salted to preserve it.

Food storage
To survive a siege, the castle inhabitants needed lots of food. Stores included hundreds of sacks of grain, which was made into flour for bread. The coolest part of the castle was the cellar, so perishable food was stored there.

Open hearth
There was no stove in the kitchen. The cooks roasted meat in front of an open fire and boiled food in huge pots.

Forging links
At the forge the armorer manufactured and repaired weapons and armor, and the farrier (blacksmith) made and fitted horseshoes.

Clever defense
Steps on the staircase always rose clockwise. This gave the defending soldier an advantage as he moved up or down. Holding his sword in his right hand, he could swing it freely. But the center post blocked the attacker's sword hand.

Well, well...
Every castle needed lots of fresh water, so there was a deep well full of fresh water.

Center post

Stables

OBSERVATORY

Through an ordinary high-powered telescope you can see mountains on the moon, nearly 240,000 miles away. The Hale telescope, however, at Mount Palomar, near San Diego, California, is so powerful that it is never pointed at anything as close as the moon. Instead, astronomers (people who study the stars) use it to look at more distant objects in the night sky. The telescope's 200-inch-wide mirror can detect stars too far away for our eyes to see. Some of these stars are so distant that their light takes millions of years to reach the earth. Looking at these stars is like looking into the past, for you are seeing them as they were millions of years ago.

Dome sandwich
A sandwich of crumpled aluminum foil lines the dome and insulates the observatory from the sun's rays during the day.

Prime focus platform
To reach the observer's cage at the prime focus of the telescope, astronomers ride in an open elevator. The elevator runs on curved rails and takes astronomers to within a step of the cage, regardless of the telescope's position.

Shutter drive and track
The shutter is so heavy that a motor is needed to open it by moving the shutter sideways along its track.

Oil-pumping equipment
The telescope rides on bearings supported by pressurized oil. Pumps collect the used oil where it flows from the bearings, and force it back to the bearings at 30 times the pressure in a car tire.

Midnight snack
Since most of the observatory's work takes place at night, the astronomers eat their main meal in the middle of the night.

The ups and downs
To look at objects higher and lower in the sky, the telescope tilts up and down. Astronomers call the degree of tilt the declination. This huge gear wheel controls the up-and-down movement.

Secondary mirrors
To focus the image from the primary mirror at points on the tube other than the prime focus, mirrors are swung into position below the observer's cage.

Crane
From time to time parts of the telescope must be removed for servicing; this is done with the help of a 67-ton overhead crane.

Dome structure
A skin of steel plates protects the telescope from the elements. A mesh of girders supports the steel cover.

Stairs

Passenger elevator

Storage area

Right ascension drive
This motor turns the telescope to change its "right ascension," so that astronomers can look left and right. Combining right ascension and declination movements enables astronomers to look at any star.

Observatory entrance

Marvelous mirror
A huge dish-shaped piece of special glass forms the primary or main mirror of the telescope. It weighs nearly 16.5 tons. The primary mirror is not a solid block: if it had been solid, cooling it after casting would have taken a year.

Mirror supports
Huge supports ensure that the mirror's shape remains correct.

Cassegrain focus
Reflected light passes back through the primary mirror and forms an image at the "Cassegrain focus." This is the most used observing position. Images are recorded by devices similar to video camcorders.

6

7

KEY FACTS

Dome diameter	• 135 feet
Mirror diameter	• 200 inches
Tube length	• 55 feet
Tube weight	• 594 tons

Field of view of telescope
The telescope gives astronomers a good view of a narrow section of the sky, indicated by shading here.

Dome wall
The dome of the telescope weighs more than 1,100 tons. It rests on wheeled trucks that run on rails around the edge of the observatory. Computer-controlled motors turn the dome to keep its opening aligned with the telescope.

Standard time equipment
Years ago, elaborate equipment was needed to measure time with the high degree of precision that astronomers demand. Today, computerized time-keeping equipment is used and takes up much less space.

Cool dome
The enclosed areas of the observatory are air conditioned.

Dome shutter
The telescope "looks out" through a 30-foot-wide slot in the dome. When the observatory is not in use, a vast shutter covers the slot.

Mounting
The horseshoe shape of the mounting enables the telescope to tilt right up to the vertical, so that astronomers can look at the sky directly overhead.

Shiny dome
Silver paint on the outside of the dome reflects the sun's heat, to help the observatory stay cool.

BIG EYES ON THE SKIES

The 200-inch reflecting telescope at Mount Palomar, in southern California, is named after George Ellery Hale (1868–1938), an American astronomer who helped plan and raise funds for the observatory. When the telescope was completed in 1948, it was the largest optical telescope in the world. The Hale telescope's size record was broken only in 1976, when the Soviet Union brought a 20-foot reflecting telescope into use in the Caucasus region. This vast telescope is so sensitive that it is capable of spotting a candle flame 14,000 miles away.

Space snaps
The large darkroom dates from the time when astronomers used photographic plates to record their observations. Nowadays most observations are recorded electronically.

Dial-a-star
Astronomers can dial in the position of star they want to look at, and the telescope moves automatically into position.

Equipment entrance
The observatory has an enormous door to provide access for heavy equipment.

Telescope cage
To keep the mirrors the correct distance apart, the Hale telescope has steel beams arranged into a long cage weighing 600 tons. If the cage were completely rigid, it would be impossibly heavy. So the cage is slightly flexible — but it is constructed so that the optical components remain in correct alignment even when the cage flexes slightly under its own weight.

Radial knife edges
Girders called knife edges support the observer's cage, but they are very thin so that they stop as little light as possible from reaching the primary mirror.

Observer's cage
In most reflecting telescopes, the observer sees the image from the primary mirror by viewing its reflection in angled mirrors positioned inside the tube. The Hale telescope is so big, however, that the astronomer can actually sit inside the tube. This position is called the prime (main) focus, because the primary mirror gathers light from the sky and focuses it (projects a clear image here).

Pressure bearings
The oil-pressured bearings reduce friction so much that even a strong gust of wind can turn the 550-ton weight of the telescope on its mounting.

GALLEON

In the 16th century, large ships regularly traveled back and forth across the Atlantic Ocean between Spain and its colonies in the New World. With their billowing sails and creaking timbers, these galleons looked and sounded beautiful. But what would it have been like for the sailors? The first thing they would have noticed when they went on board was the smell — a mixture of tar, sewage, and sweat. With a daily water ration of little more than one quart, there was not much left for washing. The ship was very crowded; there was no privacy, because every bit of space was needed for food and equipment. Huge rats scuttled in the shadows, and the ship was infested with fleas. The food tasted disgusting, and most of the crew members were constantly seasick. With a good wind, the journey from the Americas to Spain took more than two months. If the ship was becalmed (reached a patch of sea with no wind) or ran into rough weather, the journey could take even longer.

Jardines
For toilets, the crew used seats overhanging the deck rail. As a joke they called them jardines — a French word meaning "gardens."

Soldiers
On Spanish fighting ships, the crew simply sailed the vessel and did not fight. Infantry (soldiers) operated the guns and fought the enemy.

Stowaways
Thousands of rats lived on board ship. The sailors on one ship killed 4,000 rats during a voyage from the Caribbean to Europe in 1622. The rats that survived ate most of the ship's food.

Food storage
Ships carried olive oil for cooking in huge jars. Meat was usually pickled in salt water but was also hung from the deck rail, where the salt spray would preserve it. On one 17th-century voyage sharks snapped at the meat dangling above the water!

Hull
The hull, or main body of the ship, was made entirely of wood. It took hundreds of trees to build a really big wooden ship.

Ram
The carved figure on the bow (front) of the ship could be used to ram enemy ships.

Place your bets
Many sailors gambled, betting on cards, dice, and anything else that involved chance. Life on board ship for months at a time was very dull, and any activity that filled the long off-duty hours was welcomed by the ship's crew.

Swivel guns
These small guns were nicknamed "murderers." They were used against enemy sailors.

Tunes
The sailors sang special work songs called shanties. The songs had a strong rhythm which helped all the sailors to heave (pull) at the same time.

It's about time
Everyone in the crew took turns at the watch (keeping lookout). Watches lasted eight hours and were timed with an hourglass. Sand took half an hour to run through the narrow waist of this glass bottle.

Gratings
Structures called gratings let in light and air to the lower decks. They also let in lots of water.

Deck rail

Anchors aweigh!
The anchor cable ran around a huge drum called a capstan. The sailors turned the drum to raise the anchor.

An even keel
The keel was the backbone of the ship, and enabled it to sail in a straight line. To stay upright, the ship carried ballast in the hold (storage area). Rocks and cannonballs made good ballast.

Sacks of food

Water, water everywhere...
Everyone on board was allowed only one quart of water each day, or twice this amount of beer or cider. Every ship had to carry enough fresh water for the whole voyage, because sea water was too much dissolved salt to drink.

Food and cooking
Each day every member of the crew ate only 25 ounces of biscuits and 9 ounces of dried meat or fish. Sometimes there was a dish of boiled beans or peas as well. By the end of a long voyage a lot of food had gone bad, and the biscuits were filled with insects. When the sea was too rough, cooking was impossible, so everyone ate cheese instead of meat.

8